Clifford
the Firehouse Dog

Norman Bridwell

SCHOLASTIC INC.

New York   Toronto   London   Auckland
Sydney   Mexico City   New Delhi   Hong Kong

For Maxwell Bruno Wayne

ISBN 978-0-545-021580-0

Copyright © 1994 by Norman Bridwell.

All rights reserved. Published by Scholastic Inc.
SCHOLASTIC, CARTWHEEL BOOKS, and associated logos are trademarks and/or registered trademarks of Scholastic Inc.
CLIFFORD, CLIFFORD THE BIG RED DOG, and BE BIG are registered trademarks of Norman Bridwell.

Library of Congress Cataloging-in-Publication Data is available.

12 11 10 9 8   12 13 14

Printed in the U.S.A.   40
This edition first printing, May 2010
Colorist: Manny Campana

My name is Emily Elizabeth,
and this is my dog, Clifford.
Clifford is not the oldest in his family,
but he's the biggest.

Last week Clifford and I went to the city
to visit Clifford's brother, Nero.
Clifford knew the way.

Nero lives in a firehouse.

He is a fire rescue dog.

I asked the firefighters if Clifford could help them.
They thought he was the right color for the job.

Just then a group of schoolchildren came in
for a fire safety class.

Nero showed them what to do if their clothing was on fire.

To smother the flames, you stop,
drop to the floor,
and roll until the fire is out.

Clifford thought he could do that.
He repeated the lesson for the class.

He stopped.

He dropped.

He rolled.

He rolled a little too far.

Just then, we heard the siren.
There was a fire!

Nero stayed to guard the children.
Clifford and I ran ahead.

He cleared the street for the fire trucks.

Smoke was pouring from the top floor
of a tall building. Clifford pushed the crowd back
to a safe place.

He saw some people in trouble.

Clifford to the rescue!

The heavy hose was hard to unreel.
Clifford gave the firefighters a hand.

But then he saw that the fire hydrant was stuck shut.

Thank goodness Clifford was there to unstick it.

They had to get the smoke out of the building.
Clifford made a hole in the roof.

The firefighters were calling for more water.

Clifford found some.

He helped clear the smoke away.

When the fire was out, Clifford made sure that the firefighters got out of the building safely.

They were grateful for everything he had done to help.

We gave some firefighters a ride back to the firehouse.

Clifford was a hero! The fire chief made him an honorary
fire rescue dog, just like his brother, Nero.

CLIFFORD'S
FIRE SAFETY RULES

1. Tape the number of your Fire Department to your telephone.*

2. Know two different ways out of your house or apartment building.

3. Choose a place nearby where you and other members of your family can meet if you have to leave your house and get separated.

4. Never go back into your house for anything if the building is on fire.

5. Tell your mom or dad to change the battery in your smoke alarms every year on your birthday.

6. Do NOT play with matches.

7. Never use the stove without an adult.

*Some phones can be programmed to dial the Fire Department for you. Ask your parents if your phone is programmed and how it works.